For Andy,
captain of the Prestonville

SIMON AND SCHUSTER
This edition published in 2015
First published in 2013 by Simon and Schuster UK Ltd
1st Floor, 222 Gray's Inn Road, London WC1X 8HB
A CBS Company

A CIP catalogue record for this book is available
from the British Library upon request

ISBN: 978-1-4711-4416-5

Printed in China

1 3 5 7 9 10 8 6 4 2

NO-BOT

THE ROBOT WITH NO BOTTOM!

by Sue Hendra

SIMON AND SCHUSTER
London New York Sydney Toronto New Delhi

Bernard the robot loved to play at the park.

Wheeee!
He swung high, high, high,
up into the sky.

Soon it was time to go. Bernard jumped
off the swing and headed home.

He'd only walked a little way, when . . .

"My bottom!" cried Bernard.
"It's disappeared! Where can it be?"

Bernard went back to the park to look,
but he couldn't see his bottom anywhere.

"Excuse me, Monkey," he said.
"Have you seen my bottom?"

"Hmmm," said Monkey. "I think I might have. Bird is using it. Come and see!"

"Hello, Bird," said Monkey. "Have you still got Bernard's bottom?"

"Ooops, Bernard, was that your bottom?" said Bird. "It was too heavy to be a nest . . .

"Excuse me, Bear, have you been drumming on my bottom?" asked Bernard.

"Ooops, Bernard, was that your bottom?" said Bear. "It made a funny noise so I couldn't use it. I don't know where it is now."

"Oh," said Bernard.

"Don't worry. Your bottom's got to be somewhere," said his friends kindly.

"Look, there it is!" said Monkey.

"That's just Gary's hat," said Bernard.

"There!" said Bird.

"That's just Edward's shopping basket," said Bernard.

"Isn't that it?" said Bear.

"No, that's just Dog's window box."

Bernard was sad. "I'll never get my bottom back," he sobbed.

"Come and sit down," said his friends,
"and we'll think where to look next."

"I CAN'T sit down!" said Bernard.
"I haven't got a bottom!
I'm not a robot –

After a while, he arrived at the beach.
   He looked out to sea, and saw something
   very familiar.

                    There it was . . .

"Come back!" he shouted. "Come back here!
You've got my bottom!"
But the rabbits couldn't hear him.

Bernard jumped and waved but it was no good.

Then, as he turned away, he spotted
a strange-shaped sandcastle.

He had found his BOTTOM!

Bernard was so happy to have his bottom back, he did a wiggling, jiggling dance – and so did all his friends!

And Bernard never lost his bottom again.